To Live on an Island

EMMA BLAND SMITH   ILLUSTRATED BY ELIZABETH PERSON

little bigfoot
an imprint of sasquatch books
seattle, wa

Water all around. Whales out the window. Ferries passing by.
For an island kid, this is life.

Off the coast of Washington State rise hundreds of small islands. Some are lush and green. Others are rugged and rocky. And each has its own personality.

Many islands are home mostly to deer, but quite a few have farms and fields, schools and stores, and people.

What is it like to live on an island?

Well . . .

When you live on an island, the horn of the ferry is your alarm clock. To other vessels, it says, "Watch out, I'm coming through!" To you, it means, "Time to wake up, another day begins."

THE FERRIES ARE A FIXTURE of life here in the San Juan Islands. All day, they faithfully ply the waters of the Salish Sea, bringing passengers and cars from the mainland to the major islands—San Juan, Orcas, Lopez, and Shaw—and back again.

Islanders might take a ferry to see a movie or for a soccer game, doctor's appointment, or business meeting. (Talk about a scenic commute!)

When you live on an island, getting to school is an adventure. You have to hike through the woods just to reach the bus stop! Your friends scramble down dirt paths, bike, ride a moped, and even sail a boat.

KIDS GET TO SCHOOL in all different ways here. Certain islands have no schools at all, and on others, schools only go up to eighth grade. In these places, students commute daily by boat to larger islands. (Some kids even sleep away from home, returning only on weekends!)

Shaw Island's Little Red Schoolhouse was built in 1890, became a two-room school in the 1970s, and is still in use today.

BECAUSE NO SCHOOL here is far from the sea, field trips to the beach are a common occurrence. In rocky areas, when the tide rolls out, shallow puddles appear, brimming with interesting creatures.

Tide poolers can find orange and purple sea stars, sea anemones that close up lightning fast, tiny crabs scuttling for shelter, spiky sea urchins (ouch!), and dark-blue mussels clinging like glue to the rocks.

When you live on an island, you spend more time outside than in. On days when the beach becomes your classroom, you dig for sand crabs, investigate tide pools, and make the perfect belt out of a piece of silky kelp.

When you live on an island, you learn to be a builder. The giant pieces of smooth driftwood on the beach are just the thing for constructing forts. You may stop by on your way home from school to see what new treasures the sea has brought in so you can add another touch to your masterpiece.

MANY BEACHES here are strewn with massive piles of driftwood. The wood makes excellent building material for forts, and some artists use it to create whimsical sculptures on the beach. Many pieces are so big, they could actually be called drift logs, and some have been around for hundreds of years!

Where does the wood come from? It slides off bluffs and drifts down rivers and is an integral part of the ecosystem. Driftwood prevents erosion and provides a habitat for birds and small mammals.

MANY ISLAND KIDS grow up fishing for crabs. It's pretty simple. The traps are called pots, and after baiting them with delicacies that crabs love, such as raw chicken, fish heads, or cat food (yum!), crabbers drop the pots—attached to a rope and marked with a buoy—into the water. A few hours later, when the pots are pulled up, crabbers count how many they've got.

When you live on an island, you may spot your uncle and cousin out on the water checking their crab pots. "Come and help!" they call, and you do. Dinner!

BECAUSE THERE AREN'T MANY STORES here, islanders rely quite a bit on mail order. With so many deliveries, people occasionally forget what they've ordered! Every package becomes a mystery.

Getting mail can be complicated. In towns, many people have to walk to the post office to pick up their deliveries. On some islands, the mail comes only a few times a week. On others, residents boat over to the mainland for their letters. And a truly ferocious storm will keep islanders waiting for their deliveries until the weather calms down.

WALDRON ISLAND

When you live on an island, you wave at everyone who passes by, just because. But when you see the mail truck, you wave extra hard. Some days the mailman has something special for you.

STUART ISLAND

ORCAS ISLAND

SAN JUAN ISLAND

IT'S NOT UNCOMMON here for people to just drop by or even let themselves in to their friends' homes. Because the islands are small and going on or off island is such an undertaking, there is a real sense of stability and trust. People know their neighbors, and they don't hesitate to ask a favor—or to offer their own assistance.

The downside? Not a lot of privacy! There's no hanging around in underwear when a neighbor might just pop over to borrow a cup of sugar.

When you live on an island, by the time you get home, your best friend may already be waiting inside for you. You cheer! She helps you open your package.

When you live on an island, the water is your playground. After school, you head down to the lake with your friend.

KIDS SPEND A LOT OF TIME on the water here. Paddling in a lake is a great way to see aquatic wildlife—like river otters!

The sea is full of beautiful animals too. From a kayak, paddleboard, or boat, people can sometimes catch a glimpse of seals, sea lions, minke whales, humpback whales, and orcas.

When you live on an island, binoculars come in handy. There's so much wildlife to discover, like the bald eagles that live by the lake.

THE SAN JUAN ISLANDS have the greatest concentration of bald eagles in the lower forty-eight states. Bald eagles mate for life and produce one to three eggs a year. In many places on the islands, people have set up telescopes pointed right at a nest, so anyone passing by can take a peek!

Eagles like to perch high in a tree, scanning the water. A patient observer might witness an eagle swoop down and snatch up a fish. Spectacular!

When you live on an island, your grandma may fly herself over for an evening visit! She lives just a few islands away so she could take the ferry, but flying is faster.

ON THE ISLANDS, a tiny plane puttering overhead is as common a sight and sound as a ferry. Many locals have pilot's licenses and fly themselves around the islands and to the mainland. Little propeller planes whisk passengers to hospitals off island if there is an emergency, and arrive on island loaded with packages for delivery. Floatplanes are special planes that can land on water if no landing strip is available. Watching them take off is a real treat.

When you live on an island, your job may be to put away the chickens and pick veggies for dinner. (Drat—someone left the garden gate open!)

FOLKS HERE LOVE NATURE. For many, gardening and keeping animals is just another way of connecting with the environment.

But there's one big obstacle: deer! Because they have no remaining natural predators, deer have thrived on—some would say overrun—the islands. (They even swim from island to island!) Deer will destroy a garden if it's not enclosed by a tall fence—or if someone leaves the gate open. (Oops!)

When you live on an island, the power goes out a lot. But you don't mind. It's a good excuse to grab blankets, light the lantern, and play your favorite board game.

HIGH WINDS THAT BLOW through the islands sometimes knock down trees, causing an outage. Every house is stocked with candles and a good lantern.

Grown-ups might think losing electricity is a hassle, but not kids. When the power goes out early, school is canceled! It's the San Juan Islands version of a snow day (although islanders do get some of those too).

When you live on an island, you may
count orcas, not sheep, to get to sleep.

SPYHOP

BREACH

TAIL SLAP

ORCAS (OR KILLER WHALES) are a special symbol of the San Juan Islands. Three pods, identified as J, K, and L, spend the warmer months off the west side of San Juan Island. Led by matriarchs (older female leaders), they swim up to one hundred miles per day looking for salmon.

They interact in a very human way, teasing, playing, and teaching. One of their most interesting—and endearing—features is that offspring, both males and females, stay close to their mothers their entire lives. No other mammals on Earth display this behavior.

When you live on an island, things are different. Sometimes harder. Sometimes sweeter. Sometimes quieter.

Always magical.

Manufactured in China by C&C Offset Printing Co. Ltd. Shenzhen, Guangdong Province, in January 2019

Published by Little Bigfoot, an imprint of Sasquatch Books

LITTLE BIGFOOT with colophon is a registered trademark of Penguin Random House LLC

23 22 21 20 19   9 8 7 6 5 4 3 2 1

Editor: Christy Cox
Design: Tony Ong

Library of Congress Cataloging-in-Publication Data

Names: Smith, Emma Bland, author. | Person, Elizabeth, illustrator.
Title: To live on an island / Emma Bland Smith ; illustrations by Elizabeth
   Person.
Description: Seattle, WA : Little Bigfoot, an imprint of Sasquatch Books,
   [2019]
Identifiers: LCCN 2018014669 | ISBN 9781632171818 (hardcover)
Subjects: LCSH: Island life--Northwest, Pacific--Juvenile literature. |
   Northwest, Pacific--Social life and customs--Juvenile literature.
Classification: LCC GT3481.U6 S65 2019 | DDC 392.3/09795--dc23
LC record available at https://lccn.loc.gov/2018014669

ISBN: 978-1-63217-181-8

Sasquatch Books
1904 Third Avenue, Suite 710
Seattle, WA 98101
(206) 467-4300
SasquatchBooks.com

Map image is available directly from elizabethperson.com.

For Alex—there's no one I would rather explore an island with. —E.B.S.

For Mom and Dad, who gave us roots and wings. —E.P.

ACKNOWLEDGMENTS:
Special thanks to Orcas residents Mandy Randolph and Kari Van Gelder, who shared their knowledge of the islands with me; to Shaw General Store owner Terri Mason, who generously insisted on lending me her car so I could really visit the island; and most of all, to my wonderful editor Christy Cox, who made this book happen. —E.B.S.

the
San Juan
Islands